"Our Story begins with a young boy named Nicholas,
who lived in a place called Myraville,
where no one had ever heard of Christmas."

"He was an orphan child that was raised by his uncle,
who taught him the art of giving,
and to always be humble.

"The town was ruled by an evil king named Dyco, who wanted all gifts for himself, leaving none to those below.

"When he discovered that gift giving was Nicholas's action, Dyco told him to leave and stop being a distraction".

"Nicholas's uncle gave him a
charm and told him
to remember, that the art of giving
should be carried on forever"

"Nicholas found the only sailor in town,
offered him a present,
and asked if he can sail around"

"The sailor accepted and explained his plan,
to sail North with his daughter Lucy,
and be a fisherman"

"Nicholas knew that it was love at first sight, because when he saw Lucy, his heart grew bright."

"They took off while the sailor led,
looking at the ocean,
not knowing what lied ahead."

"The ship arrived on a land covered in white, the sailor grabbed his fishing rod and said, 'the fish here will be alright.'"

"The fish didn't really catch their attention,
so Lucy said to Nicholas,
'let's go look for a penguin!'"

"They spent hours searching for a penguin to find, but instead of an animal, they saw something that shined."

"They followed the bright creature's track, and to their surprise, the creature had a large pack."

13

"One creature spotted the kids hiding,
then pulled the alarm,
and they all came riding!"

"An old one informed the young <u>kids</u>,
that their species are called elves,
and he offered them <u>figs</u>."

"The wise old elf took them on a tour, showed them the village elves, and where the reindeer were secure."

"'What about over there?' asked Lucy and the elf replied, 'we do not know because the doors will not open and believe me, we've tried.'"

"But there is a tale that their ancestors once <u>said</u>, only the kindest person can put this star on top of the tree and good spirit will <u>spread</u>."

18

"Nicholas is the kindest person I know Lucy shouted! Nicholas smiled although his climbing skills he really doubted."

"It would make Lucy happy, Nicholas thought, so he put the star on his back and didn't think a whole lot."

"The elves explained how the tree can get snowy, so they gave him a hat to keep his head toasty"

"So Nicholas set out on his main goal, to get to the top of the tree, the highest place in the North Pole."

"After countless time he had finally reached the top, to put the star on the tree, and see what was up."

23

"Nicholas placed the star and felt a <u>vibration</u>, then a beam of light went through the star, and covered the tree in <u>decoration</u>."

"Everyone's spirits grew golden,
dancing and singing,
while the door finally swung open."

25

"The three led the way,
into what looked like a toy factory,
and saw a great sleigh."

"In this sleigh there was,
instructions for a boy named Nicholas,
who would forever be known as Santa Claus."

"The instructions also read,
that only through the art of giving
can Christmas cheer be spread."

"Santa Claus continued to give gifts to the world teaching people to remember, that the art of giving, should be carried on forever!"

"The End."

30

Made in the USA
Las Vegas, NV
23 October 2022

57993188R00019